New Truck on the Block

Adapted by Jo Hurley
Illustrated by Tino Santanach

ISBN 0-439-84296-4

12 11 10 9 8 7 6 5 4 3 2   6 7 8 9 10/0
Printed in the U.S.A.
First printing, August 2006

SCHOLASTIC INC.

New York   Toronto   London   Auckland   Sydney
Mexico City   New Delhi   Hong Kong   Buenos Aires

Let me tell you about the day Red came to our town, Green Meadows. Life was sunny. The sky was blue. The birds were singing.

Down at fire truck school, Chief was teaching
Petrol and Crabby how to tow cables.

"Pretend I'm trapped," Chief said.
"Use your tow cables to lasso me!"

Petrol was too nervous. He looped his hose in a tree.
And Crabby managed to wrap his hose around himself.
But no one rescued Chief.

On the other side of Green Meadows, a brand-new little fire truck named Red saw a big fire burning. He didn't know it was a practice fire.

"Woohoo, here I come!" Red whistled loudly. "Excuse me! In a hurry!" Red raced along. But he took one turn too fast.

Red almost knocked Bubba the Bulldozer off the road. "Where's the fire, son?" Bubba asked, shaking some dirt off his windshield.

"I don't know," Red said. "But as soon as I find it,
I'm going to put it out."
Red turned on his flashing lights.
"The sirens say help's on the wayyyy!" he said
as he continued down the mountain.

Red arrived at fire truck school and tossed out his
tow cable, rescuing Chief.
"Nice work, son," Chief said. "What's your name?"
"They call me Red! I want to learn to be the best
fire truck I can be!"
Chief smiled. "Welcome to the firehouse, Red," he said.

Tech the Mechanic showed Red to his new parking place.
Red was so happy to see his new room.

But Petrol and Crabby were not happy.
"He made us look really bad in front of Chief,"
Petrol said to Crabby.
"I think he's a big show-off," Crabby agreed.

From inside his garage, Red heard what the other trucks said.
It made him very sad. Red hadn't meant to make anyone look bad.
He was just trying his best.

Red rushed off to find Petrol and Crabby to tell them what had happened. But as Red drove, he went way too fast. And he wasn't watching the road. *SCREEEEEEECH!*

"Somebody help me!" Red cried.

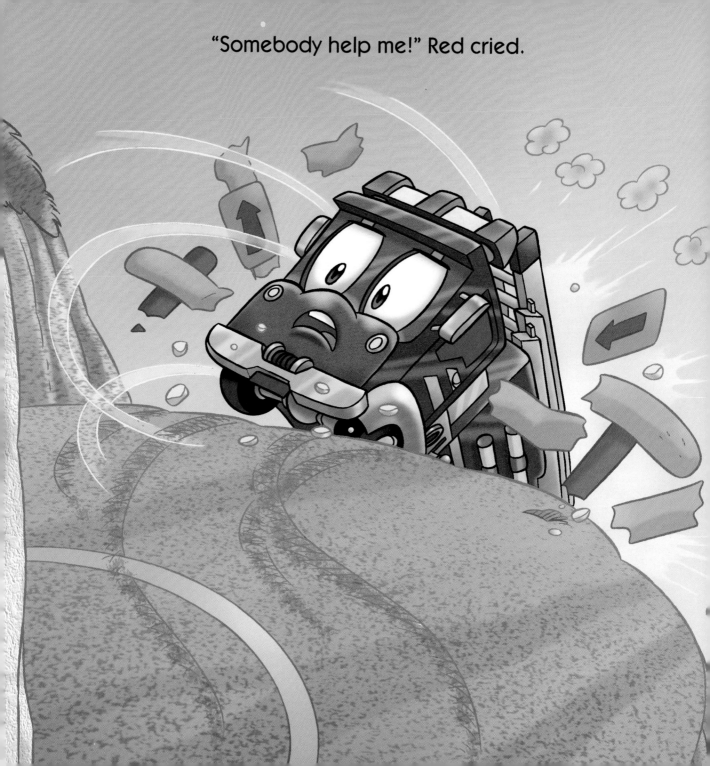

Petrol and Crabby heard Red's cries. They zoomed up the mountain and saw Red hanging off the side of the road. "We'd better get Chief!" Petrol said.

"There isn't enough time!" Red cried.
"Use your tow cables to rescue me!"

"No way!" said Crabby. "Every time I try to lasso something, I lasso me."

"Not every time," Petrol said. "Once you lassoed *me*!"

Red slipped down the mountain a little more.
Time was running out.
"You both can do it!" Red cried. "Just give it your best!"

Crabby and Petrol threw out their towlines. Unfortunately, the cables got all tangled up. "Not again!" yelled Crabby. He sounded worried.

But Red wasn't worried at all. He attached his hook to the tangled cables. Crabby and Petrol pulled — hard. In no time, Red was safe again.

"Hot stuff!" Red cried. "Thanks!"

Just then, Chief drove up, looking concerned.
"What happened here?" he asked the trucks.
"I went over the cliff, but Crabby and Petrol saved me,"
Red said, smiling.
"We did?" Crabby and Petrol asked.
"Yes, you did!" Red replied.
"Nice work, boys! You're learning!" Chief said.

"Hey, we worked as a team!" Petrol said.
"We should do that again!" Crabby added.
Red laughed. "But next time, let's do it
without me driving off a cliff!"